Contentment

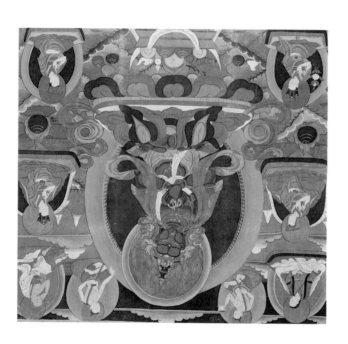

Contentment

Gillian Stokes

Red Wheel
Boston, MA / York Beach, ME

First published by MQ Publications Limited, 12 The Ivories, 6-8
Northhampton St., London, N1 2HY

First published in the United States in 2002 by
Red Wheel/Weiser, LLC
York Beach, ME
With editorial offices at:
368 Congress Street
Boston, MA 02210
www.redwheelweiser.com

Copyright © MQ Publications Limited 2002
Text © Gillian Stokes 2002
Design: Philippa Jarvis

ISBN: 1-59003-035-4

Printed in China

09 08 07 06 05 04 03 02
9 8 7 6 5 4 3 2 1

The paper used in this publication meets the minimum requirements of
the American National Standard for Information Sciences—
Permanence of Paper for Printed Library Materials Z39.48-1992 (R1997).

Permissions have been sought where possible for all quotations used.
Please contact the company for any information regarding these.

Contents

Preface

“ *The man is happiest who lives from day to day and asks no more, garnering the simple goodness of a life.* ”

EURIPIDES

Contentment is a state of grace, a state of peace and happiness, appreciation and enjoyment for what is, right now. Desires, in contrast, can never be satisfied. Once we get what we crave, we soon find it less satisfying than we expected, so we strive for something else. The only escape from this perpetual wheel of want is to discover the contentment and perfection we already have.

Contentment—a frozen moment of joy, a perfect now—will, if we allow it, expand to become a lasting expression of warmth and appreciation for the gift of life. Contentment arises when we glimpse what it means to be present in the moment with no concern for the future or anxiety over the past. We become aware of a sense of now, with how perfect that feels. Contentment wells up when we become satisfied with who we are, what we have, where we are, and that we are living by our own values. It may be fleeting; it may last for minutes, hours, or days. For the fortunate, it may last a lifetime.

Many things can trigger our awareness of contentment: the sight of a loved one, the kind actions of a stranger, the satisfaction of completing a job well, the sight of an animal's antics, the sound of bird song, the smell of baking bread or the scent of incense in a place of worship. Perhaps your joy flows at the sight of a gleaming kitchen or a fine sports car, a field of corn, a baby's smile. The trigger that initiates contentment is unique for each person.

❝ *Peace is when time doesn't matter when it passes by.* ❞

MARIA SCHELL

Contentment is a state of mind, a feeling—not the byproduct of a specific accomplishment. It does not automatically arise because we own the right "toys," though these may bring us pleasure. Nor does it come through reaching some predefined level of income, though that may bring security. It certainly has nothing to do with our status relative to anyone else's. If we imagine we can find contentment by feeling superior to another, we are doomed to dissatisfaction. The inevitability of change threatens such a precarious satisfaction. Dissatisfaction will eventually assail us after each desirable acquisition, and we will feel the need for another, and another. Desire can never quell desires. If we define contentment as a quality beyond ourselves, as something "out there" that money can buy, it will always seem elusive, fleeting. There will always be someone richer who will mar such a narrow sense of contentment. Contentment itself brings us our greatest wealth. It comes with living life well, not from a visible lifestyle.

" A sound mind and a sound body is a short, but full description of a happy state in this World: he that has these two, has little more to wish for; and he that wants either of them, will be little the better for anything else. "

JOHN LOCKE

Personal
Beliefs

> *What makes us discontented with our condition is the absurdly exaggerated idea we have of the happiness of others.*
>
> FRENCH PROVERB

Do you describe yourself by your occupation; by your nationality, age, or race; or by your gender, religion, or family? Does it depend on who has asked and where you are? Do you always answer in the same way, or does it depend on what you think someone else wants to hear?

To a large extent, the way we define ourselves, not some set of external limitations, shapes the parameters of our life. What we get from life depends as much on our attitude and self-belief as on opportunity and advantage. Too often our desire to fit in and have friends, rather than honest reflection, shapes the definition that we live by. What set of expectations do you live by? Consider how you think of yourself. Have you predetermined your expectations of life?

Do you have a hero? Ponder the qualities that person exemplifies—those that cause you to place him or her on a pedestal and leave you gazing from below. Are these superhuman qualities? Can you find them within yourself if you really look? What prevents you from feeling as proud of yourself as you are of your hero? However global your hero's influence today, he or she, too, started with a first step. Remember, you do not need to be perfect. Even heroes have their flaws; they are, after all, human. Take some time to think about what inspires you.

You have the freedom to experience difficulties or challenges, past or present, in any way that you choose. We sometimes forget or doubt this and we feel "victimized" by circumstances and histories beyond our control. Psychotherapist Roberto Assagioli beautifully described the freedom that we may all claim when he wrote of his imprisonment in Italy (see page 14). Assagioli reminds us that we are able to find contentment in the most unlikely of circumstances.

I realized I was free to take one of many attitudes toward the situation, to give one value or another to it, to utilize it in one way or another. I could rebel inwardly and curse; or I could submit passively, vegetating; or I could indulge in the unwholesome pleasure of self-pity and assume the martyr's role; or I could take the situation in a sporting way and with a sense of humor, considering it as a novel and interesting experience. ... I could make of it a rest cure or a period of intense thinking, either about personal matters — reviewing my past life and pondering on it — or about scientific and philosophical problems; or I could take advantage of the situation to undertake personal psychological training; or, finally, I could make it into a spiritual retreat. I had the clear, pure perception that this was entirely my own affair; that I was free to choose any or several of these attitudes.

ROBERTO ASSAGIOLI, *FREEDOM IN JAIL*

We may not all be blessed with as sanguine an approach to life as Assagioli, but he makes his point well. We create our own heaven and our own hell by how we interpret events. We can see the cup as half full or half empty; the choice is ours. Perhaps you have had a particularly difficult hand to play and have yet to reach a similar position of strength and equanimity.

❝ Being 'contented' ought to mean in English, as it does in French, being pleased. Being content with an attic ought not to mean being unable to move from it and resigned to living in it; it ought to mean appreciating all there is in such a position. ❞

GILBERT K. CHESTERTON

Learn to Know Nothing

66 Be content with what you have; rejoice in the way things are. When you realize there is nothing lacking, the whole world belongs to you. 99

LAO-TZU

Contentment steals over you like a blush when your daily affairs absorb you, but it remains elusive when you try to attract or trap it. No set of directions can guarantee it. Rather than striving for contentment, strive to be all you can.

Ultimately, contentment is a reflection of experience, belief, and awareness, but only when you acknowledge and honor your inner life—your soul or essence. Contentment is not a state of passivity and apathy. On the contrary, it results from becoming acutely present in the moment, whatever that moment brings. Even if your circumstances seem less than ideal, accept them without rancor or resistance and remain open to opportunities for improvement. We will never reach the point where progress becomes unnecessary. Though not a meaningful goal in itself, progress is a vital part of life. We will never attain that elusive plateau where contentment sits like a fat and happy cat. No income or status level will elevate us above all cares. Contentment has no fixed address. To be alive is to be open and vibrant, not smug and inert. We must claim contentment wherever we find ourselves at any given moment; embrace it as a part of the process, an experience as we journey, not as a destination. When we rejoice as much at seeing a bee on a flower as at receiving a large paycheck, taking delight and indifference from them both in equal measure, when we accept what unfolds for us without prejudice, then we enjoy contentment.

Barriers to Contentment

Clean Out the Closet

66 We are so accustomed to wearing a disguise before others that eventually we are unable to recognize ourselves.99

FRANÇOIS, DUC DE LA ROCHEFOUCAULD

*D*o you have a secret self? A self more private, and perhaps more vulnerable to criticism, than your public self? Perhaps you secretly relish your artistic nature or musical ability. Do you privately identify more with your family's heritage than with the culture in which you live? Are you a twin who longs to be recognized as an individual? Do you see a marked difference between the person you offer to the world and the one you truly believe or wish yourself to be? Contentment does not lie in practicing any specific set of actions, but you should consider whether you are living your life, or the life you believe that others expect you to live. You may see a huge difference between them. If you spend most of your time and effort fitting yourself into a suit made for someone else, it should not come as a surprise that it rarely feels comfortable and that contentment proves elusive.

In acknowledging your deeper self you will tap your capacity for enthusiasm and delight. Maybe you cannot completely replace your outer mask with your inner dreams, but can you acknowledge and incorporate both? Perhaps you can practice your heart's desire as a hobby, or take classes, or start a part-time job that allows you to explore the hidden side of your nature. Perhaps you can volunteer somewhere that will at least feed your need for self-expression even if it does not provide an income. Honor your dream. Think laterally. The accountant who aspires to acting might volunteer on the weekends as a tour guide and practice projecting her voice and pleasing a crowd. While thinking of herself as an actor who works as an accountant, and doing both jobs to the best of her ability, who knows what useful

66 *Always stay in your own movie.* 99

KEN KESEY

contacts may develop? Such contacts will certainly not beat a path to her door if she's at home watching television. She might even look for theatrical opportunities within her paying job—by giving wonderful presentations, for instance.

See life as filled with opportunity, not as filled with roadblocks. As you reorient your thoughts and beliefs, you will change your experiences. How can you gain contentment if you habitually seek out life's negatives? Listen to your hidden self; it offers precious hints about where your contentment lies.

Maybe you are one of the lucky few, living out your dream. More likely you have found sensible and practical reasons why your two worlds must remain separate. Secret dreams may be a way of compensating for the life we feel we must lead, or for our lack of self-confidence. We may fear that the world might not accept our hidden self as readily as it does the mask we present. Take a moment to consider whether this is so and why. What would you put on the line by living your dream?

What do you risk in buying that instrument you have always longed to play? Perhaps you fear failure or ridicule? As adults we can feel pressured to perform well at all we do, especially if we have children in our care, yet through failure we can gain the experience that creates good judgment. How will those in our care learn the wisdom of this lesson if not through our example? When we learn from all we experience, without favoring the good over the bad, we become wise.

If you secretly nurse artistic dreams, what might happen if you enrolled in a class or took up a sketchpad and pencil to draw what you see right now? Maybe your first attempt will not reach the perfection you'd prefer, but every great artist has to begin somewhere and most artists work through test pieces before clarifying their expression. The only failure lies in giving up altogether. Where conviction leads, expertise will likely follow. Poets should write poems; artists should produce art. Whether anyone else sees, hears, or even likes the work is not important. Contentment envelops us when we do what brings us joy.

What Is Your Problem?

66 *If you want to be happy, be.* 99

HENRY DAVID THOREAU

*C*onsider what you must change to increase your present level of happiness. What immediate effect would such a change create? Would you gain a greater sense of contentment from taking a different approach to your life or in believing that your contentment depends on external circumstances? Must you really change anything that you already do or don't do? Is it even reasonable to do so? Could it be that you are fine, right now? Do you really have a "problem," or have you shouldered responsibility for situations that are beyond your control? Do your attempts to maintain control over events prevent you from appreciating the contentment that is ever-available?

Try the following experiment. Make a list of all the things in your life that you could reasonably expect to be contented with, and then make a list of those things that you wish were different. You will not necessarily come to experience contentment through reasoning, but preparing these lists can offer an opportunity to reflect on and reappraise your life. By becoming consciously aware of the good and bad, you will gain the chance to remove the barriers to your happiness.

66 Contentment is not the fulfillment of what you want, but the realization of how much you already have. 99

ANONYMOUS

Quite often we continue to react to negative influences long after they have stopped, simply because the reaction has become an unquestioned habit or a part of who we believe we are. This exercise may provide you with a useful snapshot of your life. Perhaps you will discover some issues you can resolve, or at least improve, with some concentrated attention. Do you continue to hold on to negative reactions to old events? If your reactions no longer serve you, perhaps you can begin to release them.

66 *The world is so full of a number of things, I'm sure we should all be as happy as kings.* **99**

ROBERT LOUIS STEVENSON

The following lists may give you some ideas; you will create your own, more personal selection.

Reasons for cheerfulness:

- Good health.
- Loving relationships.
- The support of your family.
- The joy of your children.
- A satisfying career.
- An adequate income when many people have none.
- A warm and secure place to live.
- A good mind and plenty of mental stimulation.
- The comfort and loyalty of pets.
- Interesting hobbies.
- Citizenship in a great nation.
- Good neighbors.

Matters for review:

- Uncertain health.

- Unemployment or unsatisfactory employment.

- Unhappy childhood memories.

- Less than ideal housing.

- Unpleasant neighbors.

- Difficult relationships.

- Lack of family support.

- Difficult children.

- Money worries.

- Boredom.

“A man should always consider how much more unhappy he might be than he is.”

JOSEPH ADDISON

Physical or Mental?

> 66 *The man who removes a mountain begins by carrying away small stones.* 99

CHINESE PROVERB

To use a well-worn cliché, you will find contentment in becoming aware of yourself as a human being, not as a human doing. No magic formula will cause contentment to flow, but you may discover clutter and obstacles that have prevented you from recognizing contentment. We will take a look at some of these now.

What do you believe keeps you from experiencing contentment? Is there a tangible, physical reason perhaps, such as an illness that causes you pain? Have you lost a loved one? Maybe you don't like your housing conditions. Is it difficult to find work, or has your current job lost its charm? Perhaps you must live your life at such a pace that you truly have no time to allow yourself to experience contentment. Are you exposed to the constant sound of a radio or television in the background, distracting your thoughts? There are so many possible physical barriers to contentment, some of which you can alleviate, some not.

Pain, emotional or physical, can get in the way of contentment, yet there are no particular outer circumstances that definitely rule out its possibility. The capacity of the human spirit to soar despite appalling external circumstances might amaze you; inspiring stories arise from sick rooms and death beds, even from the concentration camps of the Second World War. Just as no situation rules contentment out, neither does any set of conditions make it so. No step-by-step manual will guarantee contentment. You must feel it. Contentment does not reside beyond the individual somewhere, to be found, collected, or bestowed. The best place to be is right here and right now. The only trick is to know that.

Negative attitudes can be harder to overcome than physical barriers. If we have become greatly attached to material things, we may never

66 *A man is about as happy as he makes up his mind to be.* **99**

ABRAHAM LINCOLN

feel satisfied—new things will always come along for us to crave. With this attitude, no single possession will give us contentment. When asked whether a rich man could enter the kingdom of heaven, Jesus replied that it would be as likely as a camel passing through the eye of a needle. Cravings and possessiveness form a barrier to knowing heaven, even if it waits at our door. Furthermore, the chance of gaining spiritual insight in such a life grows smaller by the minute.

When we harbor anger or resentment, great anxiety or sadness, we shut out the possibility of joy, but we cannot always see things as clearly as others might. Imagine trying to mend the hull of a boat while at sea. Sometimes it takes an outsider's perspective to help us to reframe our situation, to see the bigger problem. A person not embroiled in the emotional or physical problems that we suffer may have enough distance to throw us a lifeline: some suggestion to ease our situation or a way to find peace within it. Often physical and mental problems go hand in hand. Solve one and the other may diminish as well. A positive attitude can help us to rise above such problems, whether personal or environmental, and improved physical circumstances affect our mood.

Give some thought to the emotional issues that prevent you from experiencing contentment; you may find a way to lighten their load. Consider how you might improve your practical problems, too. Can you make your work situation better? Can you brighten your home or move to a more pleasant location? Remember to make some time for yourself amid your hectic schedule, and honor it. Pamper yourself in some way, however trivial, but try to avoid becoming a slave to cravings. Buy an occasional bunch of flowers or chocolate and a magazine, perhaps, or spend an evening out with your friends or at a sports event. What does your spirit hunger for?

> *We will discover the nature of our particular genius when we stop trying to conform to our own or to other people's models, learn to be ourselves, and allow our natural channel to open.*
>
> SHAKTI GAWAIN

What Do You Have to Lose?

66 One does not discover new lands without consenting to lose sight of the shore for a very long time. 99

ANDRÉ GIDE

Until we accept that loss can touch our life, but that in all probability we will survive it, we run the risk of living a half-life that is driven by fear and anxiety. Attempting to control the uncontrollable and to shut out what must be acknowledged will drain our energy and sap our potential for contentment. To experience the new, we must let go of the old, and to experience the future, we must let go of the past, believing fully that no real loss is involved. In return we are creating a free space into which new people and new things can flow. Change happens as a natural part of life. When we cling to people or possessions, we block and deny them the freedom to move and develop and change.

Of crimes — none is greater than having many desires.

Of disasters — none is greater than not knowing when one has enough.

Of defects — none brings more sorrow than the desire to attain.

Therefore, the contentment you have when you know that you have enough, is abiding contentment indeed.

LAO-TZU

Desire— To Have or To Be?

Listen Within

66 Nothing is better for a man than to be without anything, having no asceticism, no theory, no practice. When he is without everything, he is with everything. 99

RAINER MARIA RILKE

ontentment hovers just a breath away. Why do we not recognize it? Because we erect barriers. We become caught up in our anxieties, in making plans or in regretting the past, anything other than experiencing this moment in all its perfection. It seems that the act of being present and mindful is so precious a gift that we are unable to allow ourselves more than an occasional hint. Perhaps it is because we are afraid that letting go and allowing ourselves to truly *be* might engulf us with its intensity. So, like a child whose candy must be rationed, we defer our own pleasure.

We must deal with worldly cares—we cannot live in a hermit's cave—but we can find joy, real joy, in the midst of the world, in every nook and cranny of it. Do not keep contentment locked away in some high tower to visit only on holy days and holidays. Find it in the tax return as much as in the rose. Discover it in the sense you have of yourself in relation to what you see and do. Pay attention to it when it steals over you in a moment of solitude, as well as in a moment's compassion in a crowded supermarket. The spirit is everywhere. Just open yourself to the world around you, as free from acquired filters as

❝ *Contentment is natural wealth, luxury is artificial poverty.* ❞

SOCRATES

39

> ❝ *Since we cannot get what we
> like, let us like what we can get.* ❞
>
> **SPANISH PROVERB**

possible. Never mind what others have told you about what is beautiful or ugly, or who you should associate with. Contentment is not easily achieved, yet it is simplicity itself. Monks and recluses who spend years attempting to still their minds may experience contentment no more often than you or I. Attitude is all-important. Practice helps.

Contentment wells up in our communion with love—the dialogue between our spirit and the environment. No one and no thing can do this for us. What resonates and releases joy and contentment for you may not do so for me or for anyone else. Our rhythms may be quite different. When you open your heart and mind, your senses will follow their own maps.

By experiencing the world with our feelings as well as with our minds, we learn to experience contentment. We cannot "think" ourselves to contentment, that much is sure. Thought is detached; experience is anything but. So practice your feelings. Let them out to play as often as possible. Get to know and trust what they tell you, and learn to accept the consequences of where they lead you. You may find fear and anger as well as joy, of course. Until you own and accept all of your feelings, and risk that others will accept you for yourself, you will live a life with little, if any, contentment.

❝ *I throw myself down in my chamber, and I call in, and invite God, and his Angels thither, and when they are there, I neglect God and his Angels, for the noise of a fly, for the rattling of a coach, for the whining of a door.* ❞

JOHN DONNE

Honor and Pride

66 We have no more right to consume happiness without producing it than to consume wealth without producing it. 99

Have you ever experienced an unexpected courtesy that made you feel so good that you found yourself acting nicer toward others as well? Perhaps someone gave you the right of way on a crowded freeway or some other small act of generosity. Perhaps a sibling considered your needs over his or her own. You may have noticed that when you passed this generosity on, you felt better about yourself. A single honorable act can influence person after person in this way, like a loving ripple. Why not choose to always put others first? As you treat others, so you invite others to treat you. Honor has fallen from fashion in this competitive world, but if you become known for your honest dealings, you will likely reap great rewards in all areas of your life. Whatever your work, if you become known as reliable, as honest even when it gives you no direct benefit, as skilled at your craft, you will gain respect and gratitude and your position will flourish.

Take pride in your workmanship whether or not anyone else will see or appraise it. You have a limited span on this earth, why accept the mediocre? Create excellence for its own sake, or better yet, as an offering to God and the highest spiritual aspect of yourself. However humble or mundane the task before you, do it as if for someone you love with all your heart. How differently would you perform the smallest task if this were so? Learn to work with God or your favorite angel at your side and you will always give your best.

A big, tough samurai once went to see a little monk. "Monk," he said, in a voice accustomed to instant obedience, "teach me about heaven and hell!"

The monk looked up at this mighty warrior and replied with utter disdain, "Teach you about heaven and hell? I couldn't teach you about anything. You're dirty. You smell. Your blade is rusty. You're a disgrace, an embarrassment to the samurai class. Get out of my sight. I can't stand you."

The samurai was furious. He shook, got all

red in the face, was speechless with rage. He pulled out his sword and raised it above him, preparing to slay the monk.

"That's hell," said the monk softly.

The samurai was overwhelmed. The compassion and surrender of this little man who had offered his life to give this teaching to show him hell! He slowly put down his sword, filled with gratitude, and suddenly peaceful.

"And that's heaven," said the monk softly.

ZEN STORY

66 *Love is patient and kind; love is not jealous or boastful; it is not arrogant or rude. Love does not insist on its own way; it is not irritable or resentful; it does not rejoice at wrong, but rejoices in the right. Love bears all things, believes all things, hopes all things, endures all things.* 99

ST. PAUL: 1 CORINTHIANS 13:4–7

Authenticity

It is in this solitude that we discover that being is more important than having, and that we are worth more than the result of our efforts.

HENRI NOUWEN

How often do you perform one activity while half attending to another? Do you spend your time racing around in your car with a cell phone clamped to one ear and the car stereo blaring into the other? Do you try to read while listening to the radio, eat while watching television, or otherwise act without fully focusing your attention? If you allow mental "static" in, you will likely miss the contentment that awaits, just a breath away. Spiritual teachers advise that when you cook, you only cook; when you dig in the garden, dig in the garden. You cannot receive and transmit on the same channel.

Nowadays you may need to multitask to function in your hectic life. While this is an admirable talent, if you want to make contact with stillness and joy, you must be fully present in all activities. You do not need to avoid worldly tasks, just approach them fully awake. As a Zen saying reminds us, "Before enlightenment, chop wood, carry water— after enlightenment, chop wood, carry water." The tasks will still need doing. You do not have to live in a cave on a mountaintop to realize spiritual contentment, but if you have become habituated to noise and bustle, you might find it easier to reach a sense of contentment in a less hectic environment, at least in the beginning. The monastic life developed as a way to allow some the luxury of supportive surroundings for spiritual quests. Learn to become open-minded and aware in performing your tasks. Like a cat at a mousehole, allow yourself to relax but remain acutely attentive; contentment may steal upon you anywhere.

Have you noticed that when you focus on an activity with your whole heart and mind, time seems to stop? At such times we lose all

> **66** *I expect to pass through life but once. If, therefore, there be any kindness I can show, or any good thing I can do for my fellow being, let me do it now… as I shall not pass this way again.* **99**
>
> WILLIAM PENN

sense of self. Such authentic attention can make the simplest task an act of devotion and bring you serenity and joy. Choose a day, or perhaps just an hour. In that time, become acutely present in all that you do, using each of your senses. Later, consider how this focus altered the quality of your experience. Learn to empty yourself so contentment and serenity may fill you.

- When you listen to someone speak, offer your full attention; don't allow your mind to wander. Concentrate fully on the speaker rather than on composing your response. Observe the speaker's face and tone of voice. Truly listen.
- When you find yourself alone, listen to the sounds around you. Do you hear birds singing? Dogs barking? Children laughing? Traffic

noise? A baby crying? Has someone left a radio or television on?

- When you talk, whether to an audience of many or one, do not become distracted by the environment or by fear. Concentrate on what you have to say, and simply say it.

- When you look around, really see what the world has to offer. Artists learn to look critically at things rather than superficially, as most of us do. What do you see at this moment? Perhaps this book and your hand. Have you ever really looked at your hand? What lies beyond this book? If you had to draw or describe what you see in order to save your life, how much more attention would you give your surroundings?

- When you eat, pay attention to the sensation of food in your mouth— its texture and flavor. What does hunger feel like? What satisfies it?

- Focus on the smells around you. Do you detect pleasant aromas? How about unpleasant odors? Can you identify them?

- How does your body feel at this moment? Do you have any discomfort? Are you warm enough? Too warm? Hungry? Thirsty?

66 *Behold! I do not give lectures on a little charity. When I give, I give myself.* 99

WALT WHITMAN

66 *Do not seek fame. Do not make plans. Do not be absorbed by activities. Do not think that you know. Be aware of all that is and dwell in the infinite. Wander where there is no path. Be all that heaven gave you, but act as though you have received nothing. Be empty, that is all.* 99

CHUANG TSU

This practice forces us to slow our pace somewhat; you may be surprised by how intense the smallest act can become when you give it your full attention.

Once you become adept at keeping yourself in the moment with each of your senses, try an exercise in opening yourself generally. Pick a time and place that offers no distractions. You may choose to sit or lie down indoors, or you may prefer to walk outdoors. At first, attempt this exercise alone. Do not try to direct your experience. Let your body tune in however it chooses. Make this an exercise in allowing. Although you control your body—you choose where to settle or which direction to walk—let your mind go. Just be authentic, open, and willing to witness this moment and those that follow. Breathe naturally. If your mind wanders, allow that too. Trust in the natural rhythm of events, and allow your heart to open. Experience pure consciousness and contentment. Surrender to the moment.

> A man must be able to cut a knot, for everything cannot be untied; he must know how to disengage what is essential from the detail in which it is enwrapped, for everything cannot be equally considered; in a word, he must be able to simplify his duties, his business and his life.
>
> HENRI FREDERIC AMIEL

Goals Without Plans

> ❝ *Most people pursue pleasure with such breathless haste that they hurry past it.* ❞
>
> SØREN KIERKEGAARD

*D*o you plan and structure your workday, your vacation time, your life? These useful tools can serve us well. However, if we rely completely on calculating and planning, we will miss many of the surprises life has to offer. Consider the benefits of a little chaos. The unexpected, the unplanned-for event, can make a day, a trip, or a life, special. Such moments often bring contentment with them. If we could plan such feelings, we could package and market them; but contentment remains elusive.

The very essence of contentment is its capacity to sneak up on us. Its value cannot be outlined in any guidebook or distilled on a to-do list. When we tightly schedule our lives in an effort to maintain control, we rule out chance, and with it, life-enhancing spontaneity. In such a regimented life, how will we discover hidden talents or find ourselves delighted by the unexpected?

To approach a day, a vacation, or life with a more open approach, plan for the essentials, but allow for possibilities. Interesting diversions, unexpected opportunities, surprise meetings, happy accidents, and even disappointments may make all the difference. When you allow schedules to relax, serendipity may introduce you to inspirational alternatives that you may never have imagined.

Let me share a few contented personal memories:

I will always savor the time I met a fascinating older woman by pure chance. We and several others had appointments with an optician, who was unfortunately delayed. His receptionist directed us to a nearby café to await his arrival. The lady of my tale worked as a cat-sitter to raise the funds to travel the world. She was about to journey to South America, alone, to view the temples of the Incas and witness the

Contentment

magnificent Monarch butterflies as they mass prior to migration. When in England, she swam in a London river every single day, breaking the ice when necessary to swim during the winter months. This woman remains an inspiration to me for her fearless attitude toward solitary travel. I have never felt so contented during a lengthy wait for an appointment.

❝A journey is a person in itself; no two are alike, and all plans, safeguards, policing, and coercion are fruitless. We find after years of struggle that we do not take a trip; a trip takes us.❞

JOHN STEINBECK

Another such magical moment occurred during a highly scheduled trip to Paris. My companion wanted to see all of the sights in our limited time, so he prepared full itineraries for each day. The sun had set by the time we made our way to the last item on his must-see list, a small sculpture park on the left bank of the Seine. As we walked along the embankment opposite the floodlit Notre Dame cathedral on a warm summer evening, we were surprised to encounter fifteen or twenty people dancing the tango. They had taken advantage of the natural amphitheater formed by the embankment steps. Dancers filled the center, and spectators rested on the semi-circle of steps around the outside. Someone had brought a portable cassette player to supply their Latin music.

The dancers were of all ages, sizes, and backgrounds. One tiny middle-aged man danced with his face pressed to the chest of a young, statuesque blond. An older woman partnered an attractive young man. Some appeared expert, others less so. But they all gave themselves utterly to the passion inspired by the music, first advancing arms outstretched, heads conspiratorially low, then retreating, heads thrown back. Periodically a foot would flick out and back from behind a dancer with the speed of a chameleon's tongue. Heads tossed this way and that while feet stamped, like stallions smelling fire on the wind. All this gay activity happened within the night glow of the cathedral while the Seine lapped at the steps. Of course, this had not appeared on our itinerary, but it is the scene I shall always treasure. For me, it surpassed the Mona Lisa's smile, glimpsed between the massed heads of tourists at the Louvre art gallery, and the Eiffel tower, and for that matter the little sculpture park we had gone to see.

Another wonderful unscripted Parisian moment: a suited businessman crossing one of the many small squares in Paris encountered children playing ping-pong on an outdoor table. Irresistibly drawn, he took off his jacket, placed it with his briefcase on a bench, and politely joined the game. He played with spirit for ten minutes or so, then returned to his jacket, his briefcase, and his office. Pure gold.

Allow yourself to flow with the unexpected and increase your chances of discovering contentment. Organize and plan the skeleton of what you intend, then leave room for pleasant surprises; discover what the universe has made available for you.

Expectations and Disappointments

66 There are three answers to prayer: Yes, no, and wait a while. It must be recognized that no is an answer.99

RUTH STAFFORD PEALE

Do you only undertake tasks if you believe you will shine at them? Such fear-based behavior severely limits your potential to explore and play with what life has to offer, and it reinforces an already damaged self-esteem. When we take the small risk of extending ourselves, we know we may fail and we may encounter ridicule. But we will also enhance our esteem by having the courage to make the attempt. Succeeding will further bolster our confidence.

If we fail, we can view the attempt as an act of generosity and wisdom if those who respect us, particularly our children or younger colleagues, learn that failure can be okay—especially if we return undaunted to the task. Perhaps our parents could not teach this lesson. If so, the fear of failure may make us stick to well-worn tracks. But such actions come at a cost. These fears lead to lowered confidence, a life half lived, and little or no spontaneous joy.

If we never indulge our secret passion, whether painting, singing, playing a sport, climbing a mountain, or whatever, we miss the experiences that might bring us joy. If we do not explore our own aptitudes and show our children that setbacks are both a normal part of growth and survivable, the next generation will not learn that expertise only follows effort and practice. How else will our children learn to tackle a task and persevere long enough for it to become a skill? Explore those things that you suspect will make you happy. The Dalai Lama has said that learning to be happy is our primary task in life. I say happy people create happy relationships, happy families, and a happier society, much like the simple grains of sand create a beach.

Detachment and Satisfaction

❝ What makes us discontented with our condition is the absurdly exaggerated idea we have of the happiness of others. ❞

ANONYMOUS

ℳany religious disciplines teach the concept of an eternal element within that passes from life to life through many existences in a journey toward perfection. Some believe we choose each life before we are born. By selecting the parents and circumstances likely to provide the experiences we need, we advance ever nearer to perfection. Others believe our actions in previous lives determine our current circumstances.

" *Attachment is the source of all suffering.* **"**

BUDDHA

Those with such beliefs have no reason to feel aggrieved at difficult times. We will have preselected the experiences we suffer, however harsh, to test our mettle. If we believe in the concept of Karma, as Hindus and others do, we have invited present experiences through our past actions. People who hold such deep religious beliefs may find contentment in the harshest of situations. Believers in Christianity and Islam consider that all we endure is the will of God, or Allah, and so we should be contented with our lot. Service to a higher being often brings contentment to those who have faith.

The Buddha taught that our attachments cause us to experience suffering. We can become attached to anything imaginable—tangible or intangible. For example, we may feel attached to our identity, to who we think we are, or to our race, gender, color, ideal weight, religion, or philosophy. We might form attachments to habits—both those we consider bad and those that make us feel proud; to what we imagine we possess and fear we may lose, including life itself; to those with whom we have relationships; to the past events that shape our life, good and bad. This list has no end. With each attachment we form, we create the potential for suffering.

Although 30 spokes converge on the hub, it is the emptiness between which makes the cart go. Clay is used to make vases, but they are no use without the emptiness inside. There is no room which does not have doors and windows put into it, for again it is the emptiness within that provides the space for living. The physical has properties which the non-physical makes use of.

TAO TE CHING

All these things can introduce fear into our lives. We fear losing the things and people that we believe make us happier. We fear the presence of things that we believe will cause us pain. If we define life by the suffering we have experienced, we may even fear life without our habitual reactions to negative experiences: "I am afraid of ... because ..." or "I cannot do ... because of ..." If we left the shadow of these negative events, we would become free to take responsibility for our present. Such a step can understandably seem daunting. We may even become attached to unpleasant events because they bring the comfort of familiarity and provide an excuse for our behavior.

Buddhism teaches that all attachments create unnecessary suffering because they rest on the same two illusions—that suffering can be avoided, and that we can stop change. He realized the desire to cling to

> 66 *Learn to wish that everything should come to pass exactly as it does.* 99
>
> EPICTETUS

❝ *Accept the place that divine providence has found for you.* **❞**

RALPH WALDO EMERSON

what must inevitably change is the primary source of human misery and the principal barrier to contentment. He reminded his listeners that everything and every creature in the universe changes; even seemingly permanent objects, such as mountains and rivers, change all the time, though we may be in such a hurry we do not notice. Change is a natural and inevitable part of life and the world we live in.

For example, death awaits us all, whatever our station in life. No amount of money or good character can prevent it. We suffer if we deny this fact and try to control or prevent the inevitable. When we can accept death as a natural transition, we will free ourselves from the fear and suffering it evokes. The Buddha compassionately illustrated this point to a recently bereaved widow. She had asked him to lift her suffering by bringing her husband back to life. Rather than denying her request, the Buddha asked her to bring him a grain of mustard from a house that had not been touched by death. The widow set off on her errand, perhaps thinking the Buddha would use the humble grain of mustard in some magic ritual to restore her husband. But after the widow had called on many, many homes in her quest and heard how death had affected each family, she came to realize that death visits every home, whether of a pauper or a king. She soon saw that she would never find a home untouched by such loss. She had learned to accept her loss as inevitable, and in the process she realized how gently the Buddha had lead her to this knowledge. Rather than lecture her and demonstrate his superior understanding, he had given her a way to discover the truth for herself. He taught in this way throughout his life because he knew that each of us must consciously realize the truth. The widow returned to the Buddha and remained with him as a nun.

As change is inevitable, our attachments and desire for control cause us to suffer. If we constantly chase after the next thing and refuse to let go of the past, we cannot know the contentment that comes in each moment. With this in mind, take a moment to review the attachments you have formed. It is not necessary to separate from all things or people. However, by becoming conscious of where and to what or whom we have attachments, we can see them for what they truly are—transitory moments. We can then equip ourselves to let them go when the time is right. Learn to accept the inevitable and know that you know nothing.

66 Be ready at all times to accept the will of God, to accept the way which is put before you. Knowing there is no other, then meekly follow the path and trust in the great and glorious Spirit. 99

WHITE EAGLE

74

Balance and Harmony

66 *Paradise is where I am.* **99**

VOLTAIRE

*B*alance and harmony are dynamic, not inactive, states. To achieve balance and harmony, we must acknowledge and accept all possibilities, all opposing facts and feelings. Become realistic and practical in making plans, yet remain open to the unexpected; do not cling fearfully to predetermined ideas. Even "bad" things can lead to good results if we stay flexible and willing to learn. An underlying unity balances all. We may not be able to see this immediately, but its meaning may become clear to us in another time or place. Accept all the shades of reality you have the privilege to experience. A balanced life, lived in harmony, will reflect contentment.

Richard Jefferies lived from 1848 to 1887, a fairly short life by modern standards, but one touched by such sublime contentment that he felt compelled to record it in *The Story of My Heart* (New York: Longmans Green and Co., 1901 and St. Martin's Press, 1968). By chance, he discovered a way to harmonize his feelings. He tells of near-mystical experiences of contentment that profoundly influenced his life. You may have a place or hobby that reliably soothes and calms you; perhaps you have been fortunate enough to experience this quality as Jefferies did.

The story of my heart commences seventeen years ago. In the glow of youth there were times every now and then when I felt the necessity of a strong inspiration of soul-thought. ...There was a hill to which I used to resort at such periods. The labor of walking three miles to it, all the while gradually ascending, seemed to clear my blood of the heaviness accumulated at home. On a warm summer day the slow continued rise required continual effort, which carried away the sense of oppression. The familiar everyday scene was soon out of sight; I came to other trees, meadows, and fields; I began to breathe a new air and to have a fresher aspiration. ....Moving up the sweet, short turf, at every step my heart seemed to obtain a wider horizon of feeling; with every inhalation of rich, pure air, a deeper desire. The very light of the sun was whiter and more brilliant here. By the time I had reached the summit I had entirely forgotten the petty circumstances and the annoyance of existence, I felt myself, myself. There was an entrenchment on the summit, and going down into the fosse I walked round it slowly to recover breath. On the south-western side there was a spot where the outer bank had partially slipped, leaving a gap. There the view was of a broad plain, beautiful with wheat, and enclosed by a perfect amphitheatre of green hills. Through these hills there was one narrow groove, or pass, southwards, where the white clouds seemed to close in the horizon. Woods hid the scattered hamlets and farmhouses, so that I was quite alone.

I was utterly alone with the sun and the earth. Lying down on the grass, I spoke in my soul to the earth, the sun, the air, and a distant sea far beyond sight. I thought of the earth's firmness—I felt it bear me up; through the grassy couch there came an influence as if I could feel the great earth speaking to me. I thought of the wandering air—its pureness, which is its beauty; the air touched me and gave me something of itself. I spoke to the sea: though so far, in my mind I saw it, green at the rim of the earth and blue in deeper ocean; I desired to have its strength, its mystery and glory. Then I addressed the sun, desiring the soul equivalent of his light and brilliance, his endurance and unwearied race. I turned to the blue heaven over, gazing into its depth, inhaling its exquisite color and sweetness. The rich blue of the unattainable flower of the sky drew my soul towards it, and there it rested, for pure color is rest of heart. … I felt an emotion of the soul beyond all definition; prayer is a puny thing to it, and the word is a rude sign to the feeling, but I know no other. … With all the intensity of feeling which exalted me, all the intense communion I held with the earth, the sun and sky, the stars hidden by the light, with the ocean … with these I prayed, as if they were the keys of an instrument, of an organ, with which I swelled forth the notes of my soul, redoubling my voice by their power. The great sun burning with light; the strong earth, dear earth; the warm sky; the pure air; the thought of ocean; the inexpressible beauty of all filled me with a rapture, an ecstasy. … The prayer, this soul-emotion was in itself—not for an object—it was a passion. I hid my face in the grass, I was wholly prostrated, I lost myself in the wrestle, I was rapt and carried away.

Becoming calmer, I returned to myself and thought, reclining in rapt thought, full of aspiration, steeped to the lips of my soul in desire. I did not then define, or analyze, or understand this. I see now what I labored for was a soul-life, more soul-nature, to be exalted, to be full of soul-learning. Finally I rose, walked half a mile or so along the summit of the hill eastwards, to soothe myself and come to the common ways of life again. Had any shepherd accidentally seen me lying on the turf, he would only have thought that I was resting a few minutes; I made no outward show. Who could have imagined the whirlwind of passion that was going on within me as I reclined there! I was greatly exhausted when I reached home. Occasionally I went up the hill deliberately, deeming it good to do so; then, again, this craving carried me away up there of itself. Though the principal feeling was the same, there were variations in the mode in which it affected me.

66 However mean your life is, meet it and live it; do not shun it and call it hard names. It is not so bad as you are. It looks poorest when you are richest. The fault-finder will find faults even in paradise. Love your life. 99

HENRY DAVID THOREAU

Surprises

66 By asking for pleasure, we lose the chief pleasure, for the chief pleasure is surprise. 99

GILBERT K. CHESTERTON

*L*earn to enjoy surprises. The unexpected may bring opportunity or our next challenge. What does it matter if something disrupts your well-laid plans? How can you know that the unexpected will not offer greater benefit than what you had already planned? Your plans can only take you as far as your existing inspiration, imagination, and limitations. The surprise forces you to scale new heights even if the climb includes a few rocky patches. Perhaps the universe has handed you the very lessons you thought you had organized for yourself. Life is what happens to us, not what we plan.

If you complete your work well enough to be praised, do you regard it as a fluke? Do you tend to focus on the negative possibilities in a situation rather than the positive? When we do this we choose to create the negative by investing our attention in it. Have you learned to embrace some people and reject others without even meeting them— based not on who they are but simply on who you think they are? Do you love yourself?

How you respond when challenged is the measure of your humanity. Look at your own past; can you identify good things that came from what you first regarded as bad experiences? We develop our strength and wisdom through our dealings with adverse situations. Become an interested observer of life's twists and turns, not a victim of them. Make your life a vibrant dance. Learn to relish the unexpected.

❝ We are more often frightened than hurt; and we suffer more from imagination than from reality. ❞

SENECA

Work
and Reward

66*Not everything that is more difficult is more meritorious.*99

ST. THOMAS AQUINAS

We can most creatively express our instinctual nature through work, paid or unpaid. It has the potential to bring us great joy. But to do so, our work should reflect our nature. When what we do allows us to make tangible our true selves, we will know deep contentment. If we tackle each task before us to the best of our ability, we can find contentment in the results. We will have brought dignity to our labor. The work environment or equipment does not have to be perfect. Your task may be personal or public, as seemingly trivial as caring for yourself or speaking to your neighbors and coworkers. The relationship you have with everyday objects and events can become as sacred as your relationship to a place of worship. Indeed it should be more so, since we are here to live this life, not to sanctify it according to the dictates of another's doctrine.

Your work may be important or mundane in the eyes of the world. That evaluation does not matter. Producing the best work you can will bring joys greater than any monetary reward. Christian mystic Meister Eckhart understood this well:

> *All works are surely dead.*
> *If anything from the outside*
> *Compels you to work,*
> *Even if it were God himself compelling you to work*
> *From the outside,*
> *Your works would be dead.*
> *If your works are to live,*
> *Then God must move you from the inside,*

From the innermost region of the soul—

Then they will really live.

There is your life

And there alone you live

And your works live.

The outward work

Will never be puny

If the inward work

Is great.

And the outward work

Can never be great or even good

If the inward one is puny or of little worth.

The inward work invariably

Includes in itself

All expansiveness,

All breadth,

All length,

All depth.

Such a work

Receives and draws all its being

From nowhere else except

From and in the heart of God.

Not everyone has the good fortune of knowing this experience. Perhaps you find your work something you must tolerate to generate income. In these circumstances you can find contentment if you create an inner attitude of acceptance and serenity. No situation will automatically rule out or supply contentment. However, if your work strongly violates your natural instincts, it might benefit you to find more harmonious work. If you must continue to do paid work that offers you no satisfaction, look closely at your life outside of work. You may have superb skills as a gardener or homemaker, mechanic or musician. Reap the contentment these activities offer. Do not allow the wage to become the measure of who you are. If you can find a way to marry pleasure to your source of income, your life will be that much richer. In any case, find peace in your situation.

The rich industrialist from the north was horrified to find the southern fisherman lying lazily beside his boat, smoking a pipe.

"Why aren't you out fishing?" said the industrialist.

"Because I have caught enough fish for the day," said the fisherman.

"Why don't you catch some more?"

"What would I do with it?"

"You could earn more money," was the reply.

"With that you could have a motor fixed to

your boat to go into deeper waters and catch more fish. Then you would make enough money to buy nylon nets. These would bring you more fish and more money. Soon you would have enough money to own two boats . . . maybe even a fleet of boats. Then you would be a rich man like me."

"What would I do then?"

"Then you could really enjoy life."

"What do you think I am doing right now?"

ANONYMOUS

"Choose a job you love and you'll never have to work a day in your life."

CONFUCIUS

Motivation and Vision

66 One's real life is often the life that one does not lead. 99

OSCAR WILDE

We become what we believe we may become—no more, no less. But how often do we set limits by defining ourselves by the expectations of others, or by following a family tradition without question? Do you believe, since no one in your family has gone to art school, that you cannot? Do you teach, but long to dance; or work in a bank, but long to work with children? Does your family expect the first born to take charge of the family firm? Have several generations become doctors or lawyers? Perhaps you belong to a thespian dynasty and feel obliged to act when you would rather work as a therapist. When we spend too much of our limited lives in activities that do not express our soul's desire, we restrict our possibilities for contentment.

Contentment is not about achieving fame or applause. We do not have to gain recognition as the best sales clerk or lawyer. It is, however, important for you to know that you are the best sales clerk or lawyer that you can be. When you spend your days outwardly expressing your passionate commitments, then contentment is assured. Allow yourself to dream your vision of contentment. Then make that the prelude to realizing it in your life.

❝ *The logic of worldly success rests on a fallacy: the strange error that our perfection depends on the thoughts and opinions and applause of other men!* ❞

THOMAS MERTON

Creativity

> **There is a time for everything and a season for every activity under heaven.**
>
> ECCLESIASTES

*P*ositive thought is often an underused creative tool. When we use the creative imagination to anticipate our life-dreams as if we have already realized them, then the universe receives a clear signal. However, if we dwell on the reasons that we cannot fulfill our life-dreams, we will send a very different signal; one that asks the universe to oblige and confirm our negative expectations. When we anticipate negativity, we miss many of the opportunities that could lead to success. We unconsciously sabotage our chances and set up situations that confirm our beliefs.

There is a Sufi saying: "When a man wants the truth as badly as a drowning man wants air, then he will realize it in an instant." How many of us want the truth, or our dreams, that much? Do you indulge your creativity? You can always find some way to practice what you love. It may not generate an income, but when you honor the creative urge, you feed your soul.

Creativity is the soul at play. Find a way to spend some time with an activity that reflects your essence. If you love to sing, belt out your favorite songs in the shower. Better yet, join a choir and make your gift public. Do you love to write? Start that novel or short story, or keep a detailed journal. Consider submitting your work to a local newspaper or

> **❝ If we insist on being as sure as is conceivable … we must be content to creep along the ground, and can never soar. ❞**
>
> JOHN HENRY CARDINAL NEWMAN

66 *There is no failure, except in no longer trying; no defeat, except from within; no insurmountable barrier, except our own inherent weakness of purpose.* **99**

ANONYMOUS

magazine. Or offer to write the newsletter for your housing association, company, club, or church. Is your humor so topical you could perform at a comedy club or write jokes for a well-known comedian? How can you express your creative urge—through gardening, sculpting, writing poetry, painting, cooking, quilting, restoring vintage cars? Do you make room in your life to indulge this urge in some way? More important, do you share this self-expression with others? When we publicly express our creativity, we broadcast our love.

If you cannot make your creations public, offer them to God, in whatever form the highest expression of the spirit takes for you. When you offer your work to a higher power, every act becomes a joyful expression of your life. This welcomes a secret friend to your life, one who will never desert you. Return the talent, however humble, to its source and honor it as a sacred act.

The positive energy of any creative act takes the form of pure love. The world needs your creativity, your love. Imagine that God stands beside you as you work, and that all you do is for His pleasure. Acknowledge the angel at your elbow as you toil. When you share your talent with the world, know that through others, you share it with God.

If nature has made any one thing less susceptible than all others of exclusive property, it is the action of the thinking power called an idea... No one possesses the less, because every other possess the whole of it. He who receives an idea from me, receives instruction himself without lessening mine; as he who lights his taper at mine, receives light without darkening me.

THOMAS JEFFERSON

❝ We shall not cease from exploration, and the end of all our exploring will be to arrive where we started and know the place for the first time. ❞

T. S. ELIOT

Service or Servitude?

❝ The man who was born with a talent which he was meant to use finds his greatest happiness in using it. ❞

JOHANN WOLFGANG VON GOETHE

The act of service benefits the one who serves as much as the one served. When we freely give of ourselves and our time, we expand our capacity for love. If we remain awake to our common humanity and see it in everyone we meet, every act we perform becomes a service to ourselves as well as to others. "Love thy neighbor as thyself" takes on new meaning. All is one, indeed. How, then, can we consider any service as servitude?

Practice acts of kindness and service. The energy with which you choose to live affects those around you. When you dwell on ways to help others and cultivate your own positive qualities, you will find yourself inspired to perform acts of genuine service. In turn, you will be giving inspiration to others. If you live your life in constant opposition to others, if you try to force others to comply with your world view, you live with negativity and spread feelings of anger and hostility. Through our actions and attitudes we contribute to collective thinking—what C. G. Jung called the Collective Unconscious—and thereby help to create heaven or hell on earth.

66 Three things in human life are important: the first is to be kind. The second is to be kind. And the third is to be kind. 99

HENRY JAMES

66That best portion of a good man's life; his little, nameless, unremembered acts of kindness and love.99

WILLIAM WORDSWORTH

Value, Worth, and Praise

❝ *The contented man can be happy with what appears to be useless.* ❞

HUNG KO

*D*o you regularly make plans to improve your life, only to "upgrade" them as soon as you achieve them? Have you so fixed your gaze on the horizon that you miss the here and now? Setting goals is healthy and natural, but if you spend all of your time and energy striving toward future plans at the expense of the present moment, you will never feel satisfied. Another ambition, another must-have or must-achieve will always separate you from the contentment you might stop and enjoy right now.

Do you value the acquisition of status objects, those things that require the envy of others to make them satisfying? Do you crave the latest fashion in clothes, furnishings, or technology and need others to know that you possess them? If so, do the objects you acquired yesterday continue to please you today? How about tomorrow, next week, next month, next year? What would happen if you slipped behind in the style wars? Would you have to work harder to make enough money to maintain your status? Have you stopped to consider whether this effort and expense to keep up or get ahead makes you happy? Do you long to break free of the dictates of fashion? Have you tired of letting others determine what you should wear or eat, or how much money you should make? Have you added "relaxing" to your list of

**❝ *You can't have everything.*
Where would you put it? ❞**

STEVEN WRIGHT

❝ Happy the man who can endure the highest and the lowest fortune. He, who has endured such vicissitudes with equanimity, has deprived misfortune of its power. ❞

SENECA

goals—to attain at some future point? Perhaps when you have reached a particular milestone or acquired a certain object? Perhaps when you have started a family or purchased the perfect home? Does this drive hint at addictive behavior?

Most of us wish to have nice things; few of us will find merit in wearing a hair shirt or living with low self-esteem. Treating ourselves and others as valuable and worthy of the best is laudable, but not everything in life is about acquiring. Life is about process, about loving what you do, not what you have. Possessions can too easily disappear. Likewise, relying on the approval and envy of others or on keeping up with fashion can disappoint. Of what value are friends who only like you while you remain at the top? If you lose your job, suffer ill health, or fall victim to a fire or theft, you will find your very identity compromised. To rely on ephemeral goodwill and flimsy external circumstances is to depend on superficial and precarious supports. Respond to objects and clothing with your feelings, regardless of fashion. Make space for those things that cost nothing, especially if you receive them with love. Learn to appreciate goods for their intrinsic beauty, regardless of their worldly value.

> There are two kinds of discontent in this world. The discontent that works, and the discontent that wrings its hands. The first gets what it wants. The second loses what it has. There's no cure for the first but success and there's no cure at all for the second.
>
> GORDON GRAHAM

Community

&& Kindness is the golden chain by which society is bound together. &&

PLUTARCH

When we turn our love and attention outward, our efforts take on added meaning and purpose. To do our best for others can be infinitely more rewarding than focusing on ourselves. Why should this be? By interacting with others we reap the twin rewards of validation and appreciation, regardless of the outcome of our efforts. When we act with kindness and with consideration, our actions reflect the unity of the universe. We may start out to improve and extend ourselves and end up benefiting others, thereby increasing our rewards. We may act altruistically because we believe God wills us to. We may genuinely wish to serve and help others from an open heart that recognizes humanity's sameness amid difference. Community effort creates a pool of skills, ideas, and expertise that can accomplish tasks beyond our individual imaginings. When we care for the planet and our neighborhoods as we do ourselves, we make a real contribution to world peace and individual contentment.

The Wise Woman's Stone

A wise woman who was traveling in the mountains found a precious stone in a stream. The next day she met another traveler who was hungry, and the wise woman opened her bag to share her food. The hungry traveler saw the precious stone and asked the woman to give it to him. She did so without hesitation. The traveler left, rejoicing in his good fortune. He knew the stone was worth enough to give him security for a lifetime.

But, a few days later, he came back to return the stone to the wise woman. "I've been thinking," he said. "I know how valuable this stone is, but I give it back in the hope that you can give me something even more precious. Give me what you have within you that enabled you to give me this stone." Sometimes it is not the wealth you have but what's inside you that others need.

ANONYMOUS

107

Awareness

66 *The worst loneliness is not to be comfortable with yourself.* 99

MARK TWAIN

ontentment wells up from a sense of rightness with time and place and people. The author and playwright Samuel Beckett eloquently described this sense in his novel *Watt*:

He is well pleased. For he knows he is in the right place, at last. And he knows he is the right man, at last. In another place he would be the wrong man, still, and for another man, yes, for another man i t would be the wrong place again. But he is being what he has become, and the place being what it was made, the fit is perfect. And he knows this. No. Let us remain calm. He feels it. … Having oscillated all his life between the torments of a superficial loitering and the horrors of disinterested endeavour, he finds himself at last in a situation where to do nothing exclusively would be an act of the highest value, and significance.

How can we find contentment if we do not take responsibility for the gift of our own life? Have you neglected this responsibility, merely coasting along on what others expect of you? Perhaps you fall back on the excuse that we must honor our forebears or teachers. But no one can become wise by imitation. We shape our lives through risk, ethical action, and personal responsibility, not through blindly obeying orders. If we have been wisely taught, our actions, though uniquely personal, will reflect a distillation of that wisdom. That is the finest compliment to our teachers. Blind obedience denies the self.

Only when you freely choose to act honorably have you increased the sum of goodness in the world. If, instead, you make the choice to *not* act dishonorably, either from fear of reprisal or unquestioning obedience, you do not act ethically at all. Contentment arises when you know the honesty of your actions and when your compassion for others arises from free choice. This does not mean you must resent those who express an interest in your affairs or lend advice. Learning the right course of action for yourself and claiming it without confrontation is a life's work. And the benefits begin immediately. Do what you can and be who you are. You will make mistakes. Sometimes you will even fail or forget to try. No matter what, remain compassionate with yourself. Accept your mistakes and successes in equal measure. They are both part of who you are. When you truly know yourself and honor your needs, you will begin to recognize contentment. If you feel driven by external anxieties and pressures, you are least likely to be content.

Every moment and every event of every man's life on earth plants something in his soul. For just as the wind carries thousands of winged seeds so each moment brings with it germs of spiritual vitality that come to rest imperceptibly in the minds and wills of men. Most of these unnumbered seeds perish and are lost, because men are not prepared to receive them: for such seeds as these cannot spring up anywhere except in the good soil of freedom, spontaneity, and love.

THOMAS MERTON

Meditation and Contemplation

❝ In human intercourse the tragedy begins, not when there is misunderstanding about words, but when silence is not understood. ❞

HENRY DAVID THOREAU

Make time for silence. This gift has no equal in our busy world, though many people seem to fear it. Many even attempt to flood every second with audio-wallpaper. Try introducing silence into your daily routines. Does it affect how you perform your tasks or how you think and feel? Perhaps you could set aside a short period at the same time each day, say ten minutes at breakfast or early afternoon. If you are the gregarious sort, always talking to family or coworkers, or if you habitually choose to fill the background with the sounds of a radio or television, you may find that ten minutes seems very long and challenging. Observe yourself. How do you rationalize your actions in response to your feelings? Did the silence cause anger, frustration, or fear to well up? Did you become so agitated that you felt it absolutely essential to make a phone call or to hear a news report? How else do you avoid feeling uncomfortable with silence, with solitude? You may need to tell someone in advance about this exercise and enlist some support.

If you find the task difficult, ask yourself why, and monitor how you respond, but do persevere. Eventually your mind will stop resisting and quiet down. Then you will begin to experience another phase. In your silence, see what inner journeys you discover. What has the traffic of the outer world prevented you from learning about yourself? In silence you may find it easier to fully engage in an activity. Do you suddenly have more attention available? How has the quality of your listening and appraising changed? You may find yourself extending the time that you give to this exercise. Inner stillness, even in the midst of mayhem, can herald contentment.

Perhaps you will choose to take the gift of silence one step further and begin to meditate daily. You do not need special tools to meditate. Merely take the phone off the hook or switch off your cell phone, take yourself beyond the range of the doorbell, and make yourself comfortable. You may have seen pictures of meditators sitting cross-legged in an erect but uncomfortable-looking pose. If you can manage the traditional lotus position, fine, but there are many other ways to meditate. Don't waste your precious time by focusing on physical discomfort. The only thing you must bring to meditation is the intention of quieting your mind. Choose the position that best facilitates this. Perhaps that means lying quietly on the floor or sitting up straight with your back supported. Experiment and find what works for you.

Take a few deep, cleansing breaths and then breathe normally. You may find it helpful to concentrate on the breath as you draw it in and expel it. Consider how your life depends on this single process, yet how little attention you normally pay it. Do not try to breathe in any special way, just note the breath entering and exiting your body. Allow the breath to breathe you, determining its own rise and fall. At first you

❝ *You need not leave your room. Remain sitting at your table and listen. You need not even listen, simply wait. You need not even wait, just learn to become quiet, and still, and solitary. The world will freely offer itself to you to be unmasked. It has no choice; it will roll in ecstasy at your feet.* ❞

FRANZ KAFKA

may feel fidgety or overly aware of sounds or smells or other sensations that interfere with your concentration. Do not try to forcibly shut them out or become angry with them. They are a part of the process. Acknowledge them and gently let them go. Then bring your focus back to your breathing, noting its steady rhythm. As your body stills, your

mind may jump into overdrive, as though threatened by the quiet, demanding attention. With patient persistence you can learn to give up this chattering resistance. Settle peacefully into the stillness and meditate. You may choose to contemplate on a particular theme, or you might allow the process a free rein. Japanese Zen Buddhists often choose a koan or paradox, such as "What is the sound of one hand clapping?" for meditation. By focusing on such a conundrum, the mind must move beyond its habitual tracks, allowing a deeper state of awareness. Like contentment, such a state of consciousness is ever-present, though we rarely avail ourselves of it. Through the practice of stilling the mind, we realign ourselves with natural energies and tap into our own deeper wisdom. In our hectic everyday life, we block or override these avenues. Making time for regular inner attention will bring the rewards of peace, insight, and harmonious interactions with the world. It may also, at the beginning, allow repressed negativity to surface. Don't fight these emotions; silently observe them with dispassionate interest as they flicker across your consciousness, and let them go. You may be amazed at some of the deep feelings that surface, but in time, these too will become calm.

Be Here Now and Enjoy It

> *66 Each today, well-lived, makes yesterday a dream of happiness and each tomorrow a vision of hope. Look, therefore, to this one day, for it and it alone is life.99*

SANSKRIT POEM

To be present in each moment is both the most simple and the most difficult task we have in life. Most simple, because all we must do is pay attention. Most difficult, because our minds skitter about after any and every distraction, keeping us from paying attention. Let go of the temptation to control and organize everything. The world has a natural order and you are a part of it, not apart from it. Take responsibility for your life but also accept what life brings you. Complete your assigned tasks, then play. Like the scuba diver, trust that the water of life will support you, but know how to swim before you head for the bottom. Like the sky diver, have the faith to leap from the aircraft, but first strap on a working parachute. Have the discipline to learn how to function in this world. You will face challenges, but you will also experience joy.

❝ Happiness is the realization of God in the heart. Happiness is the result of praise and thanksgiving, of faith, of acceptance; a quiet tranquil realization of the love of God. This brings to the soul perfect and indescribable happiness. God is happiness. ❞

WHITE EAGLE

121

Non-judgmental Behavior

66 We cannot change anything until we accept it. Condemnation does not liberate, it oppresses. 99

CARL G. JUNG

*T*he more present to the moment we remain, the less judgmental we become. Content to witness rather than control, we can observe the mind and its many facets from a place of detachment. When we feel angry, a part within that can observe the anger dispassionately will see it rise and fade but remain untouched by it. When we feel joy, a part of us will observe the process but

not cling to it. Fear, lust, craving, hatred, love, and all other emotions are just aspects of awareness. We each have a part that remains detached and open to whatever emerges. When the mind becomes used to such freedom, previously suppressed feelings may surface. Calmly observe without judgment. Each emotion will pass like a cloud in the sky if we don't interfere. As we witness each on its journey, we realize how senseless and futile our efforts to dictate and control it have been. When we truly become present without judgment or fear, serene acceptance and deep contentment follow.

The converse is also true. If we judge ourselves harshly, condemn or punish ourselves for imagined failings, and believe we are not worthy of the good things life bestows, we undermine contentment. Learn to relax and become open. Accept yourself with the same compassion you would show a child. If you find yourself judging someone, change places mentally with that person. What do you know of his or her history and present difficulties? Would you behave any differently? Imagine what it might be like to physically change places. Approach this as an exercise in understanding, not in a patronizing spirit or pity.

Feeling and Expression

❝ I asked a very successful friend at our twenty-fifth alumni reunion of the Harvard Business School for his measure of success. He said, 'I learned to smell the roses.' ❞

ROBERT MEDEARIS

Too much of modern life demands that we rely on thought and rationality at the expense of feelings. In this age of reason we mistrust feelings, if we heed them at all, wasting a valuable resource. Feelings can seem untidy at times, but therein lies their strength. Instead of following linear and rational processes, their messiness binds us to

the world through instinct. All our passion and enthusiasm, emotion and intuition connects with reason through the vehicle of feelings. Without passion we would have no art, no love (and no hate).

Learn to allow yourself feeling. This does not mean that you should also act on every feeling. You may feel jumbled and confused, especially if a particular issue has greatly stirred your emotions. Pay attention to these feelings. In time, you may come to recognize your trigger points, and they may stir you to righteous, directed action. What makes you happy, angry, or sad? Can these feelings and your responses cause you to become a better person? When you strive for control and equanimity at the expense of your true feelings, you set up conditions that can lead to disease. Your emotions may not always make you proud, but own and accept them. They are a valid part of who you are. In locking them away, you destroy your vitality and health. If you feel angry, examine whether it is righteous anger. If so, how can you use that energy for good? You do not have a moral right to act out every feeling. Accept both discord and joy with equal interest and channel the energy they fuel into creative responses. Take personal responsibility for your life. Make the everyday sacred and the everyday will bring you contentment.

66 Many men go fishing all of their lives without knowing that it is not fish they are after. **99**

Picture Credits

cover: Liz Wright (Contemporary artist) Private Collection/Bridgeman Art Library.

pages 2 and 65: Tibetan School (19th Century) National Museums of Scotland/Bridgeman Art Library.

page 10: Paul Cézanne (1839–1906) Museo de Arte Sao Paulo/Bridgeman Art Library.

page 18: Caspar David Friedrich (1774–1840) Hamburg Kunsthalle/Bridgeman Art Library.

page 27: Chinese School (18th Century) Castle Museum and Art Gallery, Nottingham/Bridgeman Art Library.

pages 36–37: Vincent van Gogh (1853–90) Rijksmuseum Amsterdam/Bridgeman Art Library.

page 46: Utagawa Kuniyoshi (1798–1861) Fitzwilliam Museum, University of Cambridge/Bridgeman Art Library.

pages 54–55: Winslow Homer (1836–1910) Private Collection/Peter Willi/Bridgeman Art Library.

page 58: Caspar David Friedrich (1774–1840) Hamburg Kunsthalle/Bridgeman Art Library.

pages 80–81: Katsushika Hokusai (1760–1849) Christies Images/Bridgeman Art Library.

page 88: David Oyens (1842–1902) Private Collection/Bridgeman Art Library.

page 97: Karoly Ferenczy (1862–1917) Magyar Nemzeti Galeria, Budapest/Bridgeman Art Library.

page 101: Giotto di Bondone (c.1266–1337) Louvre, Paris/Bridgeman Art Library.

pages 108–109: Frederick Cayley Robinson (1862–1927) Lords Gallery, London/Bridgeman Art Library.

page 116: John Atkinson Grimshaw (1836–93) Leeds Museums and Galleries (City Art Gallery)/Bridgeman Art Library.

page 127: F. L. D. Bocion (1828–90) Victoria & Albert Museum/Bridgeman Art Library.

Text Credits & References

page 14: Piero Ferrucci *What We May Be: The Visions and Techniques of Psychosynthesis*, Turnstone Press Ltd 1982.

page 15: G. K. Chesterton, *A Miscellany of Men*, 1912, Dufour Editions, Philadelphia 1969.

pages 33, 85: Julia Cameron, *The Artist's Way: A Spiritual Path to Higher Creativity*, JP Tarcher 1992.

page 44: Extract from *Soul Food: Stories to Nourish the Spirit and the Heart*, by Jack Kornfeld and Christina Feldman, ©Jack Kornfield and Christina Feldman. Rprinted by permission of HarperCollins.

pages 48, 122: Paul Howker, *Soul Survivor: A Spiritual Quest Through 40 Days and 40 Nights of Mountain Solitude*, Northstone Publishing 1998.

page 59: John Steinbeck *Travels with Charley*, ©1962 by The Curtis Publishing Group, ©1962 by John Steinbeck, ©1990 by Elaine Steinbeck *et al*. Used by permission of Viking Penguin.

pages 83–84: Matthew Fox, *Meditations with Meister Eckhart*, Bear & Company Inc. 1982.

page 91: Thomas Merson, *The Seven Storey Mountain* ©1948, Harcourt Inc. by trustees of the Merton Legacy Trust. Reprinted with permission.

pages 110–111: Samuel Beckett, *Watt*, Grove Press 1970. With permission of Calder Publications Ltd.

page 124: David Miln Smith and Sandra Leicester *Hug the Monster*, Rider 1996. Used by permission of The Random House Group Ltd.